The Magic Sandman

Created and Written by
Auntie Kealoha

Illustrated by
Kathleen Phaneuf-Lorraine

HAMMOND PUBLISHING

Library of Congress Control Number: 00-091212
ISBN 0-9658588-5-5

THE MAGIC SANDMAN
Copyright © 2000 Hammond Publishing
Honolulu, Hawaii
Printed in China

HAMMOND PUBLISHING

For more information, write to:

Amy Hammond
Hammond Publishing
45-067 C Kaneohe Bay Drive
Kaneohe, Hawaii 96744
www.magicsandman.com

This book is dedicated to everyone who
throughout my life has believed in me.
I thank my parents, for the abundant inspiration,
dedication, motivation and the countless sacrifices.
I am especially grateful to them for
allowing me to follow my dreams
no matter how far away they led.

Dare to Dream!

One night I was watching by the moonlight
when I saw a sandman dance with delight.

I was supposed to be tucked in my bed,
but I was looking through the window instead.
To my surprise, what did I see?
A sandman doing handstands, looking at me!

I couldn't believe what I had just seen so I closed my eyes tightly and went fast to sleep.

Each night I watched him as the sun set.
He danced on the beach, but we never met.

He marched on the seashore rounding up shells.

He talked to the crabs and held races as well.

He played with the turtles and watched them go swim.

He gathered up stones and then threw them back in.

But in the bright sunlight he stood on the shore
pretending that he could not move any more.

One day I went to his side and I said,
"Why are you so still in the day
when I know you're alive and can play?"
To my surprise, he bent down to say,
"Anything is possible if you believe day after day."

From that day forward
we were friends from the heart.
Each day we grew closer.
We were never apart.

Some days
he looked happy.

Some days
he looked sad.

Then, one day I
thought he even
looked mad.

I ran to his side and sat down to play
when suddenly he said, "I must go away."

The very next day
when my friends came to play,
we built him a castle and
begged him to stay.

He said he was sorry that he had to go.
There would be no more dancing in the moonlight
or making sand angels waiting to take flight.
No more digging of holes or building bridges
because he had to go.

He said that friendship never ends
and that we would meet again.
Just before he washed away,
I faintly heard him say,
"Anything is possible if you believe
day after day."

Now many years had passed somehow
and I was on the beach again
when I came upon a sandman with a very familiar grin.
He was standing in the sunlight with a pretty lady friend
and a little baby sandman who said, "Can we be friends?"

Just behind the sandman was a bamboo, thatched-roof hut. I guessed it was his house surrounded by coconuts.

Now that I was older, I remember what he had said,
"Stars are made for wishing and that I should dare to dream."

Just because I'm older, doesn't mean I don't agree,
that anything is possible if you just believe.
I can still see him
dancing in the moonlight
and catching stars
by the tail for a
midnight flight.

The magic of the sandman is a gift you can receive.
All you have to do each day is dare to dream and
then you just believe.